# Puppy Love

By Sierra Harimann
Illustrated by The Artifact Group

## SCHOLASTIC INC.

New York    Toronto    London    Auckland

Sydney    Mexico City    New Delhi    Hong Kong

ISBN 978-0-545-28142-3

12 11 10 9 8 7 6 5 4 3 2 1                                                    11 12 13 14 15 16/0

Designed by Angela Jun
Printed in the U.S.A.
First printing, January 2011          40

"Rise and shine!" Ivy barked. It was the beginning of another day at Puppyville Manor.

Montana buried her snout in her pillow. "Is it time to get up already?" she asked. "It's still so dark outside. I wish it were spring!"

Fuji sat up in her bed and yawned. "I know," she told her friend. "I miss running outside in the park."

"And swimming and playing catch at the lake," Freddy added.

The puppies groaned as they stretched and rolled out of their beds.

Everyone headed to the kitchen for some puppy chow. Ivy looked around the table. Her friends all looked like they had a bad case of the winter blues. Suddenly, she had an idea.

"I know everyone is tired of winter, but I just thought of something to cheer us up," Ivy announced. "Next week is Valentine's Day. Let's have a party to celebrate!"

Montana perked up. "That's a great idea! We can decorate Puppyville Manor with hearts and colored streamers. And we can listen to music and have a dance contest, too!"

Freddy nodded. "Sounds great," he barked. "I can play all my new favorite songs."

Fuji wagged her tail happily. "And I *love* to dance!" she said.

"A dance party?" Ivy asked. She wrinkled her nose. "I was thinking of a tea party. We can wear pretty outfits and have cupcakes—with pink frosting! And we can lap up tea out of china cups."

"Ooh, la la!" Gigi giggled. "I *love* tea parties!"

"That sounds fancy," Clarissa agreed. "I can wear my new flowery headband."

GiGi

Clarissa

"Tea party it is!" Ivy said.

Montana frowned. "But I think a dance party would be more fun," she said. "Tea parties are boring."

"Boring!" Ivy cried. "How can dressing up and eating cupcakes be boring?"

"Ladies, ladies," Spike said gruffly. "Maybe we should have a vote."

The puppies looked at one another. A vote sounded fair. Montana and Ivy both nodded.

"Who wants to have an awesome dance party?"
Montana asked eagerly.

Spike, Freddy, and Fuji raised their paws.

"And who prefers a fancy tea party?" Ivy asked sweetly.

Clarissa and Gigi waved their paws in the air.

Everyone turned to look at Sammy.

"Which idea do you like best, Sammy?" Spike asked. "You're the only one who hasn't voted."

Sammy looked around. She didn't want to choose between her friends.

"I can't decide," she said softly. "Both parties sound like fun."

"Both parties!" Ivy said. "That's it! We'll have two parties. Montana can throw a dance party, and I'll have my tea party."

Montana nodded. "Fine with me," she agreed. "Everyone can decide for themselves which party to go to."

The puppies decided that the dance party would take place in the living room, and the tea party would be in the kitchen.

Montana and Fuji made lots of pink and red paper hearts to decorate Puppyville Manor. Then they strung up lots of streamers.

Ivy started planning her tea party, too. She got out all of her flowered teacups. Gigi agreed to make fancy cupcakes. Clarissa offered to make the tea.

Freddy and Spike made a playlist of their favorite songs for the dance party.

18

Everyone was helping out except Sammy. She was
working on a special project of her own.

The night before Valentine's Day, Montana was baking cookies when Ivy burst into the kitchen.

"Has anyone seen my PuppyPod?" she asked. "I can't find it! If it doesn't turn up, we won't have music for the tea party."

"We'll help you look for it, Ivy," Gigi said.

"Yeah, no problem," Freddy agreed. "We can split up and search Puppyville Manor."

But Montana was too busy to help. She had to find a container to store her cookies until the party.

While the other puppies searched Puppyville Manor for the PuppyPod, Montana searched for a box for the cookies.

Finally, Montana found a box and returned to the kitchen.

She sniffed the air. Something smelled strange.

"Oh, no!" Montana barked. "My cookies!"

She ran to the oven and pulled it open, but it was too late. The cookies were ruined!

Everyone gathered in the kitchen as Montana looked sadly at her burned cookies.

"Oh, no!" Fuji gasped. "The cookies!"

"I know," Montana said sadly. "Now we won't have any snacks for the dance party."

"And I still haven't found my PuppyPod, so we won't have any music for the tea party," Ivy said.

Sammy stepped forward shyly.

"I think I can solve both problems," Sammy suggested.

Everyone turned to look at Sammy.

"First, I want to give each of you something," Sammy said. Then she handed her friends the special valentines that she had made.

Roses are red
Violets are blue
Friendship is sweet
because of
puppies
like you!

"Valentine's Day is about spending time with puppies you care about," Sammy said softly. "You're all my friends, and I want to spend Valentine's Day with every one of you. We don't need to have separate parties—we can have one party with two themes!"

"That's a great idea," Freddy barked.

The next day, the puppies dressed up for the party. They ate the yummy cupcakes and drank the tea that Gigi and Clarissa had made for the tea party.

Then they hit the dance floor to the tunes that Freddy and Spike had picked for the dance party.

"This is the best party ever because of you, Sammy," Montana said over the music. "You reminded us what Valentine's Day is all about—being with the puppies you love!"

Sammy blushed.

"I'm just happy to be with my friends," Sammy barked. Montana and Ivy couldn't agree more.